Cataloging-in-Publication Data has been applied for and
may be obtained from the Library of Congress.

ISBN 978 1 4197 0463 5

Copyright © Doublebase Pty Ltd, 2012
First published by Penguin Group (Australia), 2012

Printed and bound in China by Everbest Printing Company Pty Ltd
10 9 8 7 6 5 4 3 2 1

Abrams Books for Young Readers are available at special discounts when purchased
in quantity for premiums and promotions as well as fundraising or educational use.
Special editions can also be created to specification. For details, contact specialmarkets@
abramsbooks.com or the address below.

115 West 18th Street
New York, NY 10011
www.abramsbooks.com

LITTLE ELEPHANTS

Graeme Base

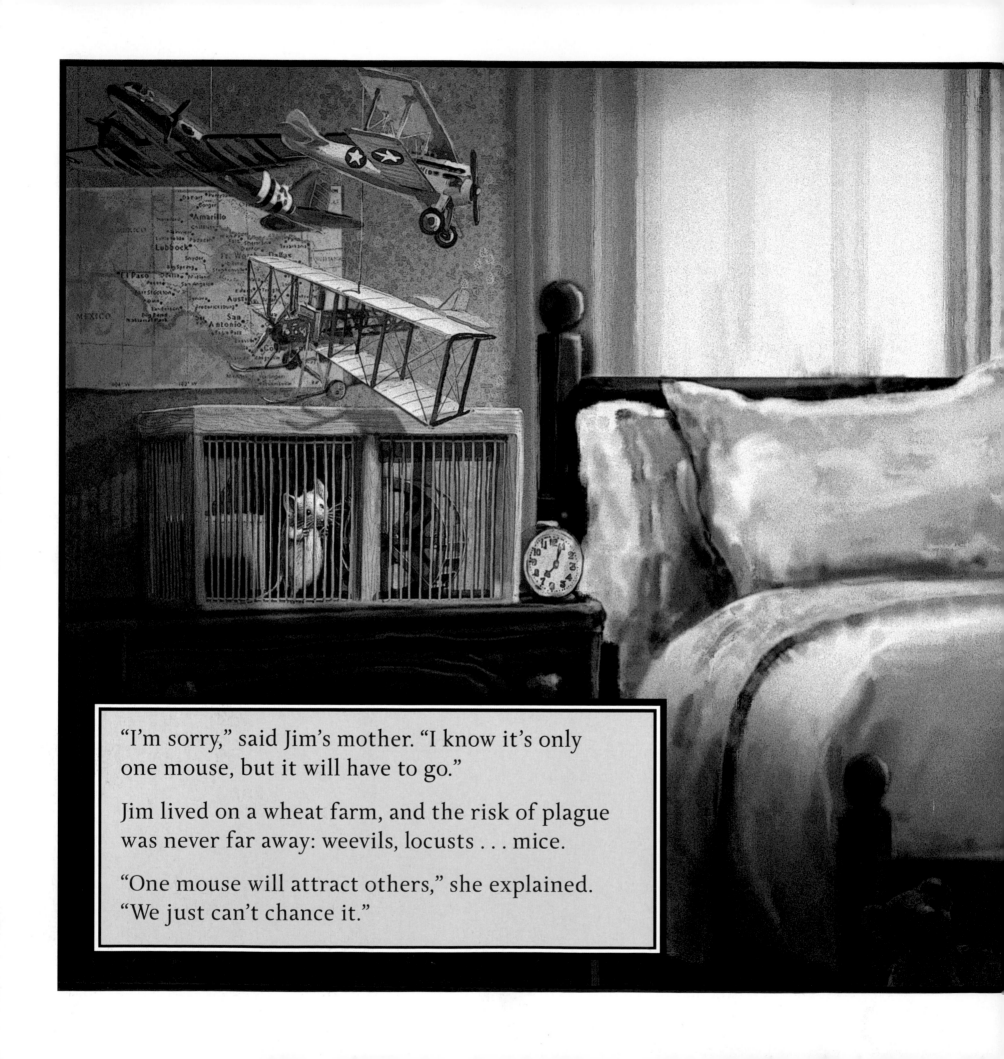

"I'm sorry," said Jim's mother. "I know it's only one mouse, but it will have to go."

Jim lived on a wheat farm, and the risk of plague was never far away: weevils, locusts . . . mice.

"One mouse will attract others," she explained. "We just can't chance it."

Jim was sad, but he understood. Times were tough, and if they lost this year's harvest, the farm would be finished.

Far from the farmhouse, he let Pipsqueak go.

When he got home, his mother was up at the workshed.

"The harvester is broken." She sighed. "I don't know how we're going to get the wheat in without it."

"We'll manage somehow," Jim promised. "Even if we have to pick it ourselves, two ears at a time."

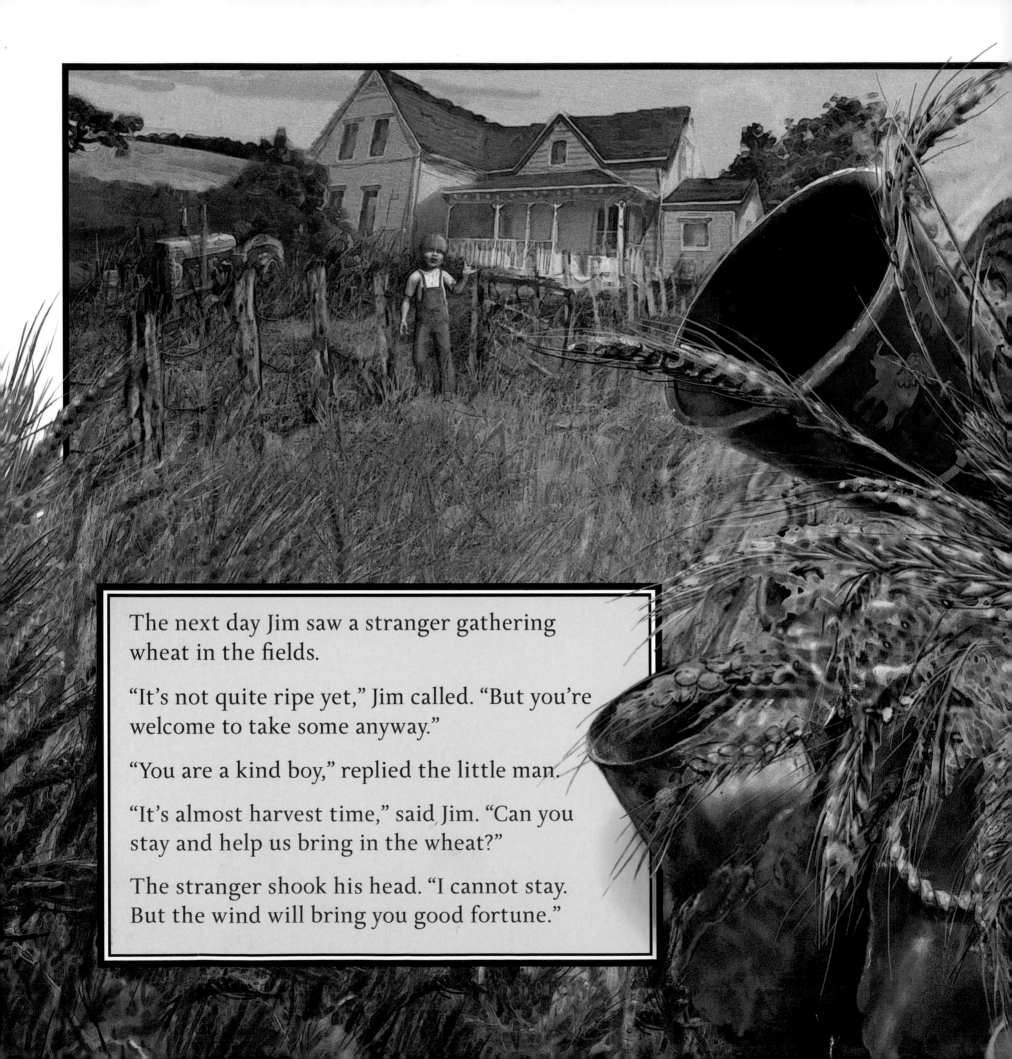

The next day Jim saw a stranger gathering wheat in the fields.

"It's not quite ripe yet," Jim called. "But you're welcome to take some anyway."

"You are a kind boy," replied the little man.

"It's almost harvest time," said Jim. "Can you stay and help us bring in the wheat?"

The stranger shook his head. "I cannot stay. But the wind will bring you good fortune."

Later that afternoon, Jim found a strange-looking horn sitting on the gate post. He blew into it, and a faraway trumpeting sound filled the air.

A shimmering cloud of gray dust wafted away on the breeze, up toward the farmhouse.

There was bad news on the radio that evening: a big locust swarm was heading their way. Jim could see that his mother was worried. If the locusts arrived before they could get the wheat in, it would be the end of the farm. The insects would eat the lot.

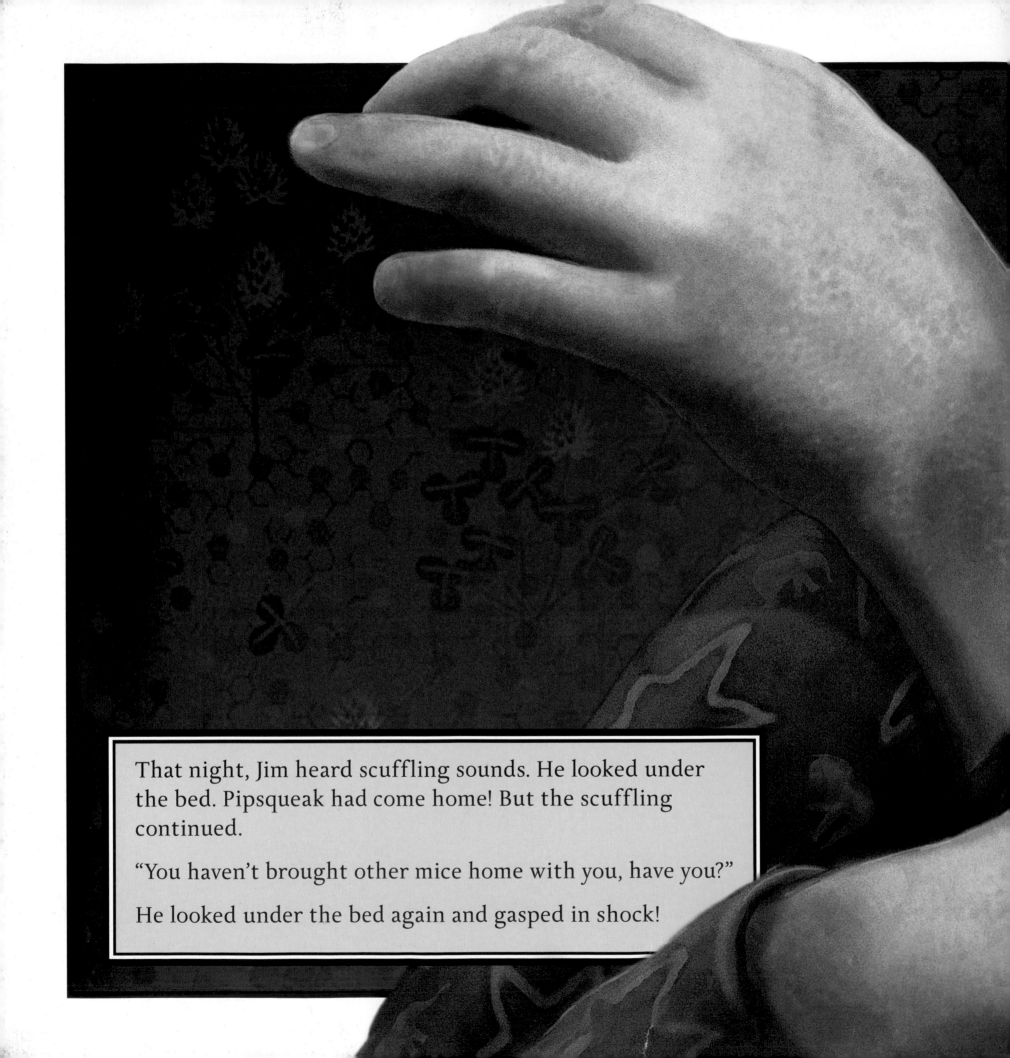

That night, Jim heard scuffling sounds. He looked under the bed. Pipsqueak had come home! But the scuffling continued.

"You haven't brought other mice home with you, have you?"

He looked under the bed again and gasped in shock!

Jim kept the little elephants secret in his bedroom. His mother was sure to think they were a plague.

But one night they escaped.

The next morning, Jim's mother looked at the kitchen floor and frowned.

"Looks like we have a mouse problem. A BIG mouse problem! Where did I put those traps?"

But at that moment there came a distant buzzing sound, growing rapidly louder. They ran to the window.

Jim and his mother looked on in despair. The locusts would destroy the wheat crop. There was nothing they could do.

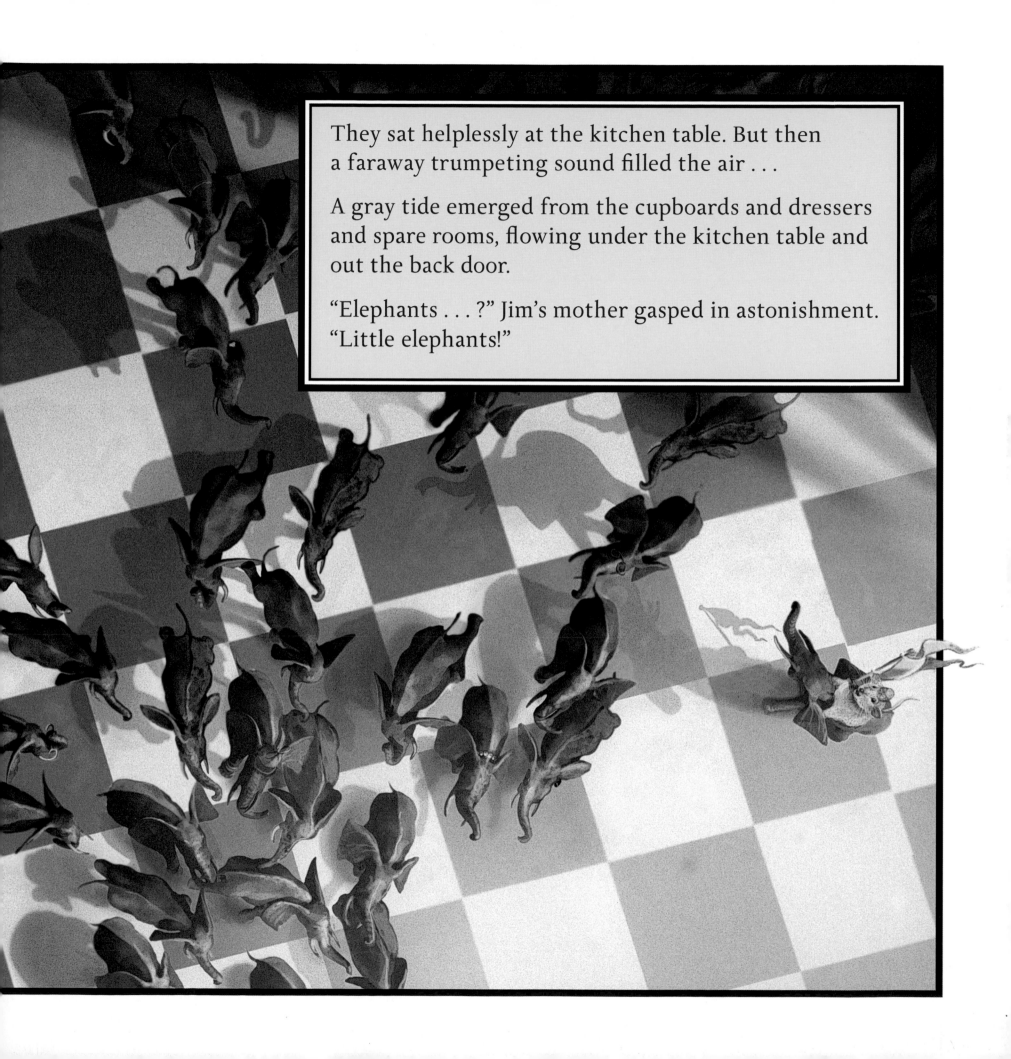

They sat helplessly at the kitchen table. But then
a faraway trumpeting sound filled the air . . .

A gray tide emerged from the cupboards and dressers
and spare rooms, flowing under the kitchen table and
out the back door.

"Elephants . . . ?" Jim's mother gasped in astonishment.
"Little elephants!"

The elephants swarmed out into the fields — and a marvelous thing happened: little wings began to sprout from their backs, and they launched themselves into the air!

At last, the locusts were driven off. Jim whooped in victory!

His mother gazed wearily across fields of golden wheat that would never be harvested. "I'm afraid it makes no difference, Jim. The wheat is ripe, but we have no way to bring it in."

But the little elephants had other ideas.

And so the harvest was brought in, just as Jim had promised . . .

Two ears at a time.